Mobo & Jill

Another Day on the Line

A short story by:

A. Ruben

Printed in the United States of America.

Mobo & Jill: Another Day on the Line / Ruben

ISBN: 978-0-9754590-6-5

Ickynicks Publishing

Front Cover by Adam Zillins

The following story is entirely fictional. Any similarity to any actual event or person is entirely coincidental and unintentional.

Acknowledgements

The author wishes to thank the following for their support: Rochelle, Lynn, Adam, Marilyn, Alex, and Sara. Thank you very much for your assistance in making this work possible.

Mobo looked at the clock. Almost time.

"So what do you think?" Dave asked, calling out to him from across the line. "Can you make it tonight? We're watching the game."

Mobo paused. What was Jill making for dinner? "I should be able to, so count me in." He hoped it was beef stroganoff, his favorite.

"Great! And hey, it's BYOB."

Mobo smiled. When was it not? Dave was his co-worker and like an old apartment neighbor he had been across from him for years; every day they punched in and took their spots on the line, working and talking. It helped pass the time, but mostly kept things from getting mundane. Dave was a hoot.

They worked for Doyle-Houser, more commonly known as DH, which designed, manufactured, marketed and distributed astronomical bodies as well as sold cosmic services. It was a very large corporation. In fact, so big was it that it consisted of multiple divisions, each developing something cosmically different, from dust to a full line of stars; DH had research and development as well as production teams, outputting anything from nebulas to white dwarf stars.

Ahead of the competition, it took a leadership role in stellar nucleosynthesis and supernovas; star production was its core nucleus and it also had subsidiaries in thermonuclear reactions, but it also mass-produced intergalactic space as well as subatomic and orbital gravity, dark energy, and mass energy.

But perhaps more importantly was its entity product line, which was as controversial as anything got. It drew mass protest from the pro-life public, whose advocates argued for instant residency of multi-cellar organisms. Proponents against that however said that evolution was an invaluable stepping-stone in shaping Life and how entities make rational decisions.

Mobo stayed out of politics... unless it dealt with the unions or his job. He was a factory worker and proud of it. His father had been on the line before him as well as his uncle. He was a second-generation and that sense of loyalty pleased him. Besides, with someone like Dave on the line who wouldn't want to come to work everyday?

2

"So Kathy tells me last night that Jill got a promotion," said Dave, adding dust into a nebula; he had to be careful. Too much and it might become a star. Kathy and Jill were as much of friends as they were.

"Yeah, I mean it's no big raise or anything," Mobo replied, "but I'm happy for her. She's had like two or three directors now, but they've been easy to work for I guess."

"That's good. Nothing worse than a lousy boss."

"Yeah that's for sure."

"So what does she do again?"

"Admin assistant. It's a legal firm."

Dave nodded. "Gotcha."

"She was telling me last night that they're going after a gas company. I guess they tried running a pipeline through a place they weren't supposed to."

"Ain't that the truth."

"What?"

"Putting your pipeline where it shouldn't go. At least that's the reason Kathy gives me every night," he winked.

Mobo chuckled. Dave was great and so was the job. It could get mundane, but really the fast-paced environment made the time fly. Everyday was a lot of the same, but never the conversation. But Mobo couldn't complain. He had been there for 19 years and enjoyed his co-workers. Management was all right. There were the good ones as well as the bad ones. Some it seemed were on vacation all the time while others were unavailable, and then there were the ones who treated the line to lunch.

"You'll never change," Mobo said, amused.

"Change isn't always good my friend. I mean after all look at what we're building."

Mobo raised an eyebrow. "What, nebulas?"

"Yes, nebulas," Dave said as if it were obvious. "Clouds of dust and gas, my friend, the pillars of creation. We're making the stuff of legends here."

"So how is that bad? That sounds pretty good to me."

"Because stuff likes stars form from them. That's why."

"You lost me. So why is that bad?"

"Stars, planets, coconuts, you know."

"Coconuts?"

"Yes, I can't stand coconuts."

Mobo snickered. "I didn't know you hate coconuts."

Dave shivered. "Uh, I can't stand it. Just the thought of it makes my whole body want to heave."

"Coconuts," he teased.

"Don't do that," he warned him with a smile. "I might actually throw up into this nebula."

"Wouldn't that be a sight, the pillars of creation… with Dave's lunch? No, but seriously, why do you think it's so bad?"

Dave paused, trying to be serious. "I guess it's the inevitability of things."

"You getting religious on me now?"

"Hell no," he said. "I'm just saying that change ultimately leads somewhere. Take the nebula. Its denser regions will condense to form a star and the remaining areas will form planets and other cosmic objects. It's something new, that's true, but then what? Maybe the star that forms is a red giant and goes supernova one day. I'd hate to be on any planet nearby."

"So what's your point, things go up as well as down?"

"Yeah, I guess. Well, I suppose that big screw-up in sales got me thinking. That's all."

Mobo hadn't heard about that. "What screw-up?"

"Oh man, I thought you knew," he said, apologizing. "Someone sold a supergiant star right beside a planet with life, and the star went supernova."

Mobo's eyes widened. "You're kidding! How'd they screw that up?" That was bad, very bad.

"I don't know man, but somebody's losing their job for sure. I mean that stuff happens right; we know that. I mean come on, shit happens, but you don't sell a planet with emerging life right next to a massive star on its way out the door. That's just bad for business."

Mobo was shocked. "How did they miss that?"

"You got me, but I tell you something I'd hate to be the person in that meeting having to explain myself."

"But it's so obvious that you don't do that. I mean, well, maybe it was a new guy. Everyone makes mistakes."

"I don't know," Dave said doubtfully. "I think it was someone trying to meet their quota or something, but whatever the reason I hear they're pulling Product Planning, Design and that assembly team leader into a meeting and you can bet your ass that team led is going to get ripped a new one. I mean if they're going to blame anyone, it'll be him."

"Do you know who it is?"

He shook his head. "I don't, but I spoke with Jerry a few days ago, you remember him. He was over in building C a couple of years back before they moved him over to D. Well, anyway, he said that he had heard that Product Planning knew about it, mentioned it to Design to fix it, but somewhere in the mess of things it all got lost in translation. Next thing you know it goes out the door and boom."

"That sucks."

"Tell me about it, but yeah listen, bring over some chips."

"Wait, what?"

"For the game."

"Uh, yeah, sure. No problem."

Dave got excited. "I tell you what, Mobo. Kathy's been watching those food shows and she's been making some good guacamole. I never thought I'd eat that stuff, but damn, if what she does isn't the best thing I've ever had."

He looked surprised. "Really?"

He nodded. "You got to get Jill to watch those shows too. I tell you what my friend. It's a marriage-saver right there. I mean Kathy's casserole is alright, but I'm not going to jump over an asteroid belt to eat it."

"I'll tell Jill about that."

"But you got to do it smoothly," he said leaning in, as if to warn him. "You may even have to watch it with her a few times, because the last thing you want is for your woman thinking she can't cook. That's a death wish, my friend. A death wish."

"I hear you," he agreed.

"And yeah, if you do end up watching those, pick the one with the barbeque or the one where they chop the cooks."

8

He jolted back. "They chop the cooks, like kill them."

"What, no! They chop them; it's a competition show. If they don't pass the judge's test then they're out. It's a good show. Get her to watch it."

"Oh, I was going to say, that didn't sound like a cooking show Jill might watch."

"Yeah, for real. No, but seriously, get her to watch it. I tell you it's seriously the best thing that's ever happened between Kathy and me." He leaned in again, "and the sex afterwards…"

"You serious?"

"Hell yes, I'm serious. I'm scarfing down what she puts in front of me, and if that's not the biggest compliment then I don't know what is."

"No shit."

"Seriously, my friend. Cooking shows. Life-saver."

Mobo smiled. Good to know he thought. Just then a hand tapped him on the shoulder. "Boss wants to see you," said a worker reliving him temporarily.

Mobo exchanged looks with Dave. Nobody was ever pulled off the line unless it was important, real important.

So, he walked down the marked aisle along the wall where yellow safety lines kept him from veering back into the assembly area. At intersections, a safety red/green light controlled traffic so forklifts could pass by; large round mirrors let him know what was around a corner when he came to an intersection. This was an additional safety precaution. At a red light, he paused briefly and waited. Then continued on.

The whole facility was dust-controlled in order to ensure quality control. He could brush his finger on a bollard and it was spotless. The only dust permitted was on the line; admittedly, it was impressive how dust-free the filtration systems kept the place, but at times it seemed like an over-kill. He came to another light, waited, and then went on.

At the tiny office, he knocked and was waved in. Inside was a small desk, file cabinet, and a boss dressed in the same sanitation outfit as him, a one-piece blue outfit that went over his clothes. His hair was shaggy and he looked stressed.

"You wanted to see me?" Mobo asked.

"Sit Mobo," the boss said, wondering how best to explain the news. Whatever it wasn't good.

"I've got good news and I've got bad news," he said, doubtfully. His voice wasn't convincing. It sounded more bad than good.

"Do I want to hear it," Mobo said, trying half-heartedly to believe there really was some good news.

His boss leaned over the desk, too drained to be tactful. "I'll be frank. You're a good worker, Mobo. You are, but my hands are tied."

Mobo sat back. This wasn't happening. His mouth opened, but he had no words.

The boss tried to soften the blow. "Listen, I said there was some good news, so let me say it."

Mobo didn't care. He went deaf to anything and everything around him. How could this be happening? Was he really being let go? He tried to deny it, but the truth just sank further down.

11

"Mobo, are you listening?" he said. "I'm trying to tell you that there's a package deal here, and if I were you I would take it."

"I'm being laid off," he said, still in disbelief.

"Look it's not my call, okay. They're outsourcing the plant and you're not the only one… Dave's in after you."

Mobo looked up in surprise. "Dave's being laid off too?"

"Everyone is."

"Yeah, but why? We do good work here," he said excitedly. He didn't understand.

"Look this isn't my call," he said, not wanting to be the bad guy. "I'm the messenger here, so put yourself in my shoes. This isn't fun for me either."

Mobo shook his head, still trying to wrap his head around what was happening. "Yeah, but why? I mean don't we get a reason, or is just about the bottom line?" His voice was rising. He felt partially betrayed. After all, he had been loyal and this was how DH rewarded him! "Tell me there's a reason."

"What do you want me to say, Mobo. That it isn't about the bottom line. Of course it is! You know that. I know that. Dave knows that; everyone does." He tried to empathize. "But what else can I say. I wish there was another reason, but it's just cheaper to produce nebulas and stars elsewhere."

"Are you getting canned?" he asked, feeling vindictive.

"Probably," his boss said. "I don't know, but that's the way the universe works, Mobo. You know that. It's what we do. Shit happens, and right now there are a million things I'd rather be doing than this. Okay? My hands are tied."

"Does this have to do with that supernova mess?"

"The what? No, that's minor in comparison," he said. "Supernovas happen all the time and worlds vanish. There's always ups and downs in business and right now I have to be the one to dish out the worst."

"Level with me."

"I am, Mobo. I'm telling you why."

"Dammit, it's the least you can do," he said, insisting on a better reason that just management's desire to improve the bottom line. "I don't care if you have to make up a reason, just give me something other than that. It's the least you can do for me." He was trying hard to control his temper. He knew it wasn't his boss's fault, but this was the last thing he wanted to hear.

"What do you want me to say? That it's a Big Freeze or the Big Crunch happening. I don't know. I'm not in accounting. I'm on the floor just like you making sure production happens like it should. I got a boss also… and more than one, which only makes my job all the more difficult."

"Yeah, it's tough being you," he said, pointing the trigger at him. What did he really care? He wasn't the one losing his job. Mobo started for the door.

"Dammit Mobo. I'm doing my best here. Take the package deal. Take an early retirement and try, just try to see that I'm trying to work with you here. Alright?"

Mobo stormed out. Security was already outside the door to escort him off the premises, which only dug the knife deeper. He couldn't even finish his shift. True, the union would ensure he got paid for it, but it didn't make things any better.

Then he thought about Jill. What was he going to tell her? How could he tell her? *Hi honey, I got fired today.* He sighed.

He stood out in the parking lot. His badge was taken, his lunchbox in hand, and even the security voice over the intercom at the gate didn't even acknowledge him; he wasn't even allowed to wave his badge at the camera. The security guard had done that for him... and then out he went, discarded like the trash.

Then it started to rain...

For what seemed like infinite, Mobo just stood there, outside DH, drenched and angry. Where was the respect? Where was the loyalty? Where was the pride that DH boasted about when it spoke about its "family of employees?" What bullshit. DH was just another corporation out to squeeze the little guy. He went to his vehicle and waited. Dave wouldn't be long; one thing was for sure nobody was probably up for game night.

His thoughts returned to Jill. What would he tell her? How could he break this kind of news to her? He sighed heavily. 19 years. Yeah sure the package deal might be good, but could he retire off it, probably not; this wasn't the first time DH had had to lay off employees, but then that's how the universe works. One day it's a big bang and the next someone in accounting makes a mistake and there's a big crunch and layoffs start happening- all because the bottom line is just that important.

He started up his vehicle. He couldn't wait for Dave. He wanted to, but he'd no doubt see him out tomorrow, maybe. Dave was good for that. Mobo could always count on him for that, but then that was when they were just having an ordinary bad day... this was a bit worse than that.

At home, Jill was waiting at home. Her eyes were drawn towards the wall, lost in a stare. Her skin was clammy and pale; clearly her day wasn't going well either.

"What's wrong, babe," he asked affectionately, hoping her news was better than his.

She stumbled to speak. "I got let go today," she said, bursting into tears. He rushed to her and embraced her in his arms.

"Ah sweetie. I'm sorry." He rocked her gently. She sobbed into his wet clothes, and then realized that he was home earlier than usual.

"Wait, why are you home so soon," she asked.

He paused, unsure how to tell her. What awful luck. As though the entire universe had turned against them today, he really didn't want to tell her. "It's nothing," he said, evading the question. "They're just switching the lines and sent a few of us home early. That's all."

After two decades of marriage, Jill knew when he was lying. She wiped away her tears. "I know you better than that Mobo, so you better be straight with me. Why are you home so early?"

What could he do? He thought about lying to her again, but the longer he hesitated the more she became upset. "I can't lie to you baby," he said, letting it off his chest. "What can I say, the universe hates us today."

She reached for him sympathetically. "Are you kidding me? Oh my goodness, no. Oh sweetie, I'm so sorry that they let you go." He didn't even need to say it. She could see it in his eyes. Pulling him into her arms, she embraced him; they were two high school sweethearts and their love was forever.

Mobo held it together though. Inside he was all torn up, but he refused to show it. He had to be strong. He had to be her anchor in this storm, He assured her that everything was going to be okay, that this wouldn't change anything and that they would find a way to keep going; but for as much of an anchor as he felt he was for Jill, he believed she was really his.

"I love you baby, and tomorrow will be better. I'll get another job. I will."

"I know you will."

"I won't let this come between you or me. I won't."

"You're a good man, Mobo, a good man. I know."

Suddenly, the phone rang.

"Now who could that be at this hour?" Jill asked, looking up curiously. She was still holding him.

"It's probably Dave," he said, pulling away, but it wasn't. Instead it was a telemarketer trying to sell share space in a solar system.

"Good evening, sir. I hope your day is going well, and I'd like to take a few moments of your time to share with you about a great opportunity to spend on a habitable planet third from its sun. It's located in a spiral galaxy and is neighbored by four gas planets and three rock planets for your enjoyment. Is this something you'd be interested in?"

Click.

Mobo cut him off angrily. Of all the nights, this was the last. He couldn't believe the nerve of that guy; telemarketers should call during the day, not at night, but apparently nobody looks at time zones; the worst were the ones with the accent though. Not only were they indiscernible, but also pestering, as if they couldn't discern your response of no thank you or good-bye; he hated telemarketers calling the house, but then who actually was eager to speak with one? He slammed the phone down bitterly, but it only made Jill snicker.

"What's so funny?" he asked, bewildered. He was upset, so why wasn't she? It wasn't like their day was getting any better.

"I love you, Mobo. Even when you're angry you're cute."

"Cute huh?"

She nodded, reaching her arms outwards towards him, beckoning him to return to her. "We both have had awful days," she said, lovingly, "but as long as I have you Mobo, I have everything."

He wrapped his arms around her. That's all he needed to hear to finish this day. What would he do without her? He paused as a frightful thought popped into his head, but then he cleared it away. No, nothing would happen to her and he wouldn't even think that way, not tonight. He just hugged her and was glad he had her. Of all the stars in the universe he had his perfect one.

She lit his path when all seemed lost. She kept his chin up and truly was his anchor; it was her resolve that gave him strength and the will to carry on. He remembered that fateful night at the school dance when he stood by the punch bowl and saw her standing alone. He was so scared, but he couldn't leave her alone during a song; it wasn't right. So he gathered up his youthful courage and asked her to dance with him. They never left each other's side after that.

Suddenly, a knock came at the door. It was Dave and Kathy as well as a few other friends. Jill and Mobo were beside themselves with surprise at the unexpected party at their door.

"Well, aren't you going to invite us in?" Dave joked. "We've all had shitty days too you know." He handed Mobo a cold six-pack. "That's yours. I've already got mine. Fuck BYOB."

It was a pleasant surprise to say the least, and Jill quickly started cleaning up. Her friend Shanice however, stopped her. "Oh don't worry about it, girl. Tonight, you and me are living it up. Now where do you keep you're limes? I brought the tequila."

"Aw shit," Ernie, her husband said half-jokingly. "You better watch yourself Jill. When she gets that in her there's no telling which direction she'll go. She might mistake you for me."

"I wouldn't mind seeing that," said Dave, smiling.

Kathy nudged him in the ribs.

Everyone laughed.

As everyone put down the plates, cups, veggies and finger food and started pouring drinks they laughed even more heartedly. "Let's get some cards going," Shanice said.

"And put the game on," Dave added. "We're making the most of this night." Mobo flipped on the tube just as the player intercepted the ball and dashed for the end zone. Everyone burst into cheers. "Alright, this night is picking up already," said Dave.

"So what are we playing," Shanice asked, cutting the deck. "Rummy, Euchre, Poker?" Kathy came over with her drink.

"Since when did you learn how to play Euchre?"

"When I was up north."

"How was it up there?"

"Cold," she said with a smile. "But quiet. It was very peaceful and relaxing, not like the hustle and bustle here."

"I need a vacation."

"So do I," Jill said lightheartedly. "But I guess I have the time now."

Shanice reached her hand out to comfort hers. "Don't worry about it tonight, girl. Let's just have fun. Tomorrow is a brand new day, and you never know what tomorrow will bring."

As the guys watched the game the girls played cards and the evening rolled by merrily. Mobo felt better by the end. Dave was good for that; Mobo thanked everyone for coming when they started to leave.

"Hey, that's what friends are for," said Ernie, giving Mobo a pat on the back. "I'll catch you real soon." Everyone wished each other a good night as they parted.

It was a good night. Their team had won and now Jill was buzzed, pulling him to the bedroom. He started to clean up, but she insisted. "Mobo! Bedroom. Now," she ordered.

"Yes, ma'am," he said, giving into her cravings. She started taking off his clothes before they were already inside. It was a great finish to a long day.

Mobo work up early, dressed, and began searching the paper for a job. He would accept the package deal, but needed something to do; it was more for Jill than him though. He looked over several jobs, from an asteroid service technician to a planetary sulfuric specialist; he passed over a photosynthesis job as well as tectonic plate mechanic. Those didn't interest him, especially the latter. It was too risky and not enough pay.

He set the paper down, feeling overwhelmed. This might take a few days. Just then though the phone rang. He quickly picked it up so as not to wake Jill. It was Ernie.

"Sorry to call you so early, man, but I was just speaking with a buddy here and he says his brother-in-law works for DH's competition and there's some openings. I figured you already had the qualifications so why not?" Ernie was a mechanic and was always at work early; he couldn't complain though. He loved to fix things and the pay was very good.

"Really?" That sounded promising.

"That's the universe for you man. Listen, here's a number to call that he gave me. You got something to write it down."

Mobo scrambled to find something. "Got it."

"Alright good. Give them a call. I gotta go."

"Hey Ernie, thanks."

"No problem. I got your back, my man. Got to run."

How about that, Mobo thought? He'd go work for the competition. DH probably didn't see that coming; it made him smile. But then Ernie was right. That's the way the universe was.